The Little Christ Child
and the
Spiders

George Buchanan

George Buchanan

Macdonald

Once upon a time, in a house near a forest lived a mother and a father, a grandmother and a grandfather, an auntie and an uncle, two children called Edward and Jane, and a dog called Benjy and a cat called Sooty.

5

The children were very excited. For days now everyone
had been getting ready for Christmas, and the house had
been given such a cleaning and a polishing as never was.
And there had been such a cooking and a baking as well,
and the most gorgeous spicy, Christmassy smells had
found their way into every corner of the house.
Edward and Jane had a lovely sticky time making

HEAPS of coloured paper chains, which they looped around the walls and across the rooms. Sprigs of holly were tucked behind the picture frames and a big bunch of mistletoe hung in the hall.

Now it was Christmas Eve, and tomorrow would be the Little Christ Child's birthday.

That afternoon, the children went with their father,
grandfather and uncle to find the most beautiful

8

Christmas tree in the forest. They carried it home
through the snow on a big toboggan.

Now it stood, tall and green in a big tub in the sitting room window, waiting for the grown-ups to decorate it after the children had gone to bed.

Long after they were in bed, Edward and Jane could hear all sorts of interesting noises downstairs. They could just see their Christmas stockings hanging at the foot of their beds. It was all so exciting that they thought they would never go to sleep, but of course, at last they did.

The grown-ups had such fun decorating the Christmas tree! Finally, Father climbed the step-ladder and fixed

the big star to the topmost branch. And so at last, the
tree was finished, ready for Christmas morning.

Uncle carried the step-ladder out to the woodshed whilst the others tidied away the boxes and the tissue paper and string. Granny put the guard around the fire, and

turned out the lights. Soon, everyone in the house
was fast asleep, and it was all quiet, and dark
and still . . .

Presently, into the house came the Little Christ Child,
to see that all was well.

He went into the downstairs rooms and saw how bright and clean they were. He saw the Christmas tree with its

18

toys and candles. He went into the kitchen to see
Benjy and Sooty. And then he went upstairs.

The Little Christ Child was just going into the
first bedroom when he heard a strange sort of
twittering noise.

It seemed to be coming from the very top of the house,
so he climbed up the dark, twisty stairs and went into
the attic. And what do you think he saw?

SPIDERS! Lots and lots of them. And they were all talking and crying and arguing as hard as they could.

"What is the matter?" asked the Little Christ Child.

So, sniffling and snuffling, the spiders told him how every year when the house was made specially clean and shiny for his birthday, they were all turned out of their nice, warm, cosy homes downstairs. And in the sitting room there was a great big SOMETHING called a Christmas

22

tree. They had one every year and the spiders were longing to see it. The grown-ups had seen it, Benjy and Sooty had seen it, the children would see it tomorrow and they were the only ones who had never, EVER seen it – and it wasn't fair!

"Well," said the Little Christ Child, "if you are very good and very quick, I will let you go and *look* at the Christmas tree, but you must promise me *not to touch*!"

23

The little spiders promised faithfully and scuttered away downstairs as fast as their legs would carry them. The Little Christ Child smiled to himself and thought "Poor little spiders!" Then he went into the bedrooms to see that all was well with the family.

When he came out, he couldn't see any spiders anywhere and he thought how very good and quick they had been. But before he left the house, the Little Christ Child thought he had better make sure those little spiders hadn't touched anything, so he went into the sitting room. And what *do* you think he saw?

That beautiful Christmas tree which the grown-ups had decorated so lovingly was covered from top to bottom with . . . spiders' webs! The spiders had been so excited to see the Christmas tree that they had quite forgotten their promise and now there they were, climbing all over it, swinging down from branch to branch, and simply covering it with their grey, dusty cobwebs.

"Oh, you naughty little spiders!" cried the Little Christ Child. "Come down at once! Oh dear, what am I going to do?"

The little spiders scuttered down the tree as fast as they could and stood in an unhappy huddle near the door.

The Little Christ Child stood and looked
at the Christmas tree and thought . . . and
then he had an idea. He went up to the
tree and gently, very gently, ran the tips of his
fingers along those grey, spidery webs. And when
he had finished, he stood back and looked at it.
"Yes," he said, "I think that will do."

The Little Christ Child smiled at the spiders.
"Thank you, little spiders," he said. "Happy
Christmas!" And he went out into the night.

The spiders gazed at the tree in amazement.
Had they really helped the Little Christ Child
to do this special magic? Then, whispering to each
other about what they had seen, they scuttled
back to their own warm, cosy homes once more.

Christmas morning came at last!

Edward and Jane rushed in and out of all the bedrooms
singing, laughing and shouting, "Happy Christmas!"
and "Can we see the tree now?"

Everyone gathered outside the sitting room, Father
flung open the door and they all crowded inside.

What a sight met their eyes! All those grey spidery webs had turned into long, shining, shimmering silver strands. For a while they were too astounded to move. Then, a little cautiously at first, they went up to the tree and gently touched the sparkling threads.

"Oh, how beautiful!" they said. "But what are they and how did they get there?"

Nobody knew. But we know, don't we?
And so, of course, did the spiders!